Clifford THE BIG RED DOG

Clifford®
Saves the Whales

Clifford THE BIG RED DOG

Clifford®
Saves the Whales

by Josephine Page
Illustrated by Carolyn Bracken and Jim Durk

**Based on the Scholastic book series
"Clifford The Big Red Dog"
by Norman Bridwell**

SCHOLASTIC INC.

New York   Toronto   London   Auckland   Sydney   Mexico City
New Delhi   Hong Kong   Buenos Aires

Library of Congress Cataloging-in-Publication Data

Page, Josephine.
    Clifford saves the whales / by Josephine Page; illustrated by Carolyn Bracken and Jim Durk.
        p.   cm.
    Summary: When Emily Elizabeth and her classmates go on a field trip, she calls on her dog Clifford to try to save some trapped whales..
    ISBN 0-439-37306-9 (pbk.)
    [1. Dogs—Fiction. 2. Whales—Fiction. 3. School field trips—Fiction 4. Wildlife rescue—Fiction.] I. Bracken, Carolyn, ill. II. Durk, Jim, ill. III. Bridwell, Norman. IV. Title.
PZ7.P1415 Ch 2002
[E] — dc21   2001049317

        10 9 8 7 6 5 4   04 05 06

Printed in the U.S.A.
First printing, May 2002

Clifford Saves the Whales

Contents

A Big Red Dog   9

Clink and Clank   13

"Sorry, Boy"   18

From the Ferry   20

A Good Swimmer   22

Not a Fish   25

There She Blows!   30

Watching Whales   33

Trapped!   40

A Red Speck   46

A True Story   57

About Whales   61

Where the Whales Are   64

🦴 A Big Red Dog

It was the day of the class trip. Miss Carrington's class was going on a whale watch. And everyone was excited.

The class rode away in a big yellow bus. Not far behind was a big red dog.

"Go away, Clifford," Jetta said.

She didn't like the big red dog. But the other kids did—especially Emily Elizabeth. The big red dog belonged to her. And every day, she was thankful for having such a special pet.

But Clifford wasn't always big. When he was born, he was smaller than all of his brothers and sisters. He was so small that Emily had to feed him with a baby doll's bottle. He was so small that the smallest dog collar was too big for him.

And he was always getting lost. He got lost in Daddy's shoe. He  got lost in Mommy's purse. He even got lost in Emily Elizabeth's cap.

At night, Emily Elizabeth would tell Clifford she loved him. She would wish that Clifford would grow to be a big, healthy dog.

And he did! Clifford grew and grew and grew. He grew bigger than a horse. He grew bigger than a house!

Now Clifford was too big for the apartment where Emily Elizabeth's family lived. And he was too big for the crowded streets in the busy city where they lived. When Clifford went for a walk, he would cause a traffic jam. So the family moved to Birdwell Island, where Clifford would have lots of room to run and play.

 Clink and Clank

Suddenly, the yellow bus began to clink and clank. It rumbled and roared. And then it stopped.

The boys and girls and their teacher got out of the bus.

"Our trip is ruined," said Jetta.

"No, it's not," said Emily Elizabeth. "Cliiiiiiifford!" she called.

Luckily, Clifford was close by. The big red dog quickly came to the rescue.

"Lie down, boy," she said.

And he did.

Starting at his left paw, Emily climbed the big red dog. She held  onto his thick fur and pulled herself up until she reached his back. Miss Carrington and the other children followed Emily Elizabeth.

Of course, no one would think of climbing up a normal-sized dog

or sitting on its back. But Clifford
wasn't a normal-sized dog.
Not at all!

So the class rode away on the
big red dog.

From high up on Clifford's back, Miss Carrington and her class had a great view of Birdwell Island. They could see the center of town—the library that was shaped like a boat, the Seashell, where Emily's mother worked, and the car wash. They could see past the park to the treetops of the forest. And they could see Samuel's Fish and Chips Shack and the carousel at the harbor.

Birdwell Island was a beautiful place. And it was a special place. It was a place where everyone

knew one another. It was a place
where, most of the time, everyone
truly cared for one another.

🦴 "Sorry, Boy"

Clifford carried the children to the pier where a ferry waited for them. They were greeted by Victor and Pedro, who owned the boat.

One by one, the children got on board. The last to board was Emily Elizabeth. Close behind her was Clifford.

Emily knew what was on his mind.

"Sorry, boy," she said to Clifford. "You can't come with us. You have to go home now."

Clifford whined and turned away. He walked toward the ferry building. But he didn't go any farther. He sat and watched as the ferry pulled away from the dock.

From the Ferry

From the ferry, Emily Elizabeth saw Birdwell Island get smaller and smaller. The steep cliffs at Rock Point looked like little stones. The lighthouse looked like a piece from a model train set. And Clifford looked like a small red puppy again.

Birdwell Island no longer looked like a place where real people lived. It looked like a toy, then a

tiny speck. Then it disappeared.
The ferry was surrounded only
by water.

Emily joined the rest of the
class. The children were having a
wonderful time. They sang songs.
They played games. They had
snacks.

From time to time, they saw other
boats—a fancy yacht, a sailboat,
even a fishing boat. The class
waved to the people on
the other boats. The
people on the other
boats waved back.

A Good Swimmer

After an hour of seeing water and boats, the children were restless. They were eager to see their first whale.

"I'm bored," said Jetta.

"Look over there!" shouted Charley.

"Is it a whale?" asked Miss Carrington.

"No," said Charley. "It's Clifford!"

And so it was. Clifford was swimming toward the ferry. Before long, he was right behind it.

Emily Elizabeth laughed. "Clifford loves the water," she said.

"He sure is a good swimmer," said Charley.

"That big dog will scare away the whales," said Jetta. "Make him go home!"

"I'm very sorry, Clifford," Emily said to the big, sad dog. "But you have to go away now."

So Clifford swam away to where he wouldn't scare the whales.

🦴 Not a Fish

"This is so boring," Jetta said. "I wish we could go back right now. Who cares about seeing a bunch of big fish anyway!"

"Whales are not fish," Miss Carrington explained. "Fish breathe through gills. That's why they can spend their whole lives underwater. That's why they can't live if they're out of the water."

"But whales can't stay underwater. They don't have gills. They have lungs—just as we do. Whales have to come up for air or they will die.

"A whale breathes through a blowhole on the top of its head. When a whale breathes out, a fountain of water vapor shoots into the air," said Miss Carrington.

"A blowhole is like a nose," said Charley.

"That's right," said Miss Carrington. "And  whales are like humans in other ways, too. Both whales and humans are mammals. Dogs are, too. Mammals have hair on their bodies—though whales and people have very little hair. And mother mammals make milk that they use to feed their babies."

"The blue whale is the largest animal alive," said Charley. "It's bigger than twenty elephants!"

"That's even bigger than Clifford!" said Emily Elizabeth.

"Yes, it is," said Miss Carrington. "I don't expect to see any blue whales today. But if we're lucky, we may see some humpback whales. They're about the same size as Clifford."

Just then, Emily felt a little sad.  Clifford would have enjoyed seeing animals that were as big as he was, she thought.

"Humpback whales make beautiful sounds," Pedro said.

"Some scientists believe that humpback whales speak to one another.

"Every year, humpback whales make a long trip. They travel from cold waters, where there is lots of food, to warm waters, where whale babies are born. Then the whales go back again." Pedro gave a sigh.

"For many years, whales were hunted. The number of whales in the world got smaller. Now many people worry that, after a while, no whales will be left."

🦴 There She Blows!

All of a sudden, the boat got very shaky. The kids slid to the left. Then they slid to the right.

"Look over there!" Charley shouted again.

"It's a whale!" said Emily Elizabeth.

"A humpback!" said Miss Carrington.

Everyone crowded along one side of the boat. In the distance was a misty spray.

Then it was gone.

About ten minutes later, the
shiny, gray back of a humpback
whale appeared in the water. Water
vapor came out from its blowhole.

Then the gray back curved into the water until only the whale's tail was left above the surface. In an instant, the tail sliced into the ocean, and the whale was out of sight.

"Wow!" said Charley. "That was exciting!"

"Exciting?" said Jetta. "All we got to see was the back and the tail. That's not exciting to me."

~ Watching Whales

Soon another humpback whale appeared just below the surface, churning up the water.

"It's a bubble cloud!" said Victor.

"This is rare," Pedro said. "We can see the whale eating!"

Miss Carrington explained how a humpback whale prepares its

dinner. "A whale blows a bubble cloud under a school of fish. The fish get trapped among the bubbles. The whale opens wide and takes in a giant mouthful of fish and water. It squeezes the water out through bristles around its mouth. Then it swallows the fish and kelp that are left."

"That's our old friend, Dotty," Victor said. "Pedro and I have seen her here many times."

"How can you tell?" Emily Elizabeth asked.

"By her tail," Pedro explained. "Each whale has its own special markings on its tail."

"Come here! There are more whales over here!" Jetta called from the other side of the boat. "A big whale and a little whale. It must be a mother and her baby!"

The class watched as the mother and baby whales swam around the boat and then under the boat.

"They're playing with us!" said Emily Elizabeth.

"They like us!" said Charley.

"Do you know them?" Emily Elizabeth asked Pedro.

Pedro waited until the mother whale came to the surface again. He could see the sleek surface of her back and the mist spouting from her blowhole. When she dived back into the water, Pedro looked carefully at her tail.

"That's Happy!" he said. "We named her Happy because the markings on her tail look like a big smile. What do you know! Happy had a baby!"

Happy and her baby were underwater for a long time. When

they came to the surface, they
were far away. They dived again.
When they resurfaced, they were
close to the ferry. And then they
dived again.

   The class waited for a long

time. But Happy and her baby didn't reappear.

"Where are they?" Jetta asked.

"It's impossible to say," Miss Carrington explained. "They could be far, far away."

"Or they could be right under our boat!" said Pedro.

Time passed. No more whales appeared.

"This is getting boring again," Jetta said. "Can we go home now?"

"Be patient," said Charley. "I have a feeling that something exciting is going to happen."

 Trapped!

A fishing boat was in the distance. As the ferry got closer to the fishing boat, the class could see that something was wrong. A whale was trapped in a net. It was Happy! She was hanging upside down next to the boat. And her blowhole was underwater.

Panicked, the baby whale swam around and around.

Victor called to the fishing boat on his radio. "You have an endangered animal inside your net."

But the captain of the fishing boat didn't answer.

"Happy will drown if she can't come up for air," Victor said.

The ferry drew closer to the fishing boat.

"You have an endangered animal inside your net," Pedro repeated. "You'll have to cut the net."

But the fishermen didn't want to cut the net. They needed the net to catch fish. If they couldn't

catch any fish today, they wouldn't
make any money.

They wouldn't be able to pay
for their food, their rent, their
heat, and other important things
their families needed.

"I wish Clifford were here," said
Charley. "I know he could do
something to help."

Emily tried to call him.
"Cliiiiifford! Cliiiiifford!"

He was too far away to hear her.

The other children joined her—
as did Miss Carrington, Victor, and
Pedro. "Cliiiiifford! Cliiiiifford!"

The loudest voice of all
belonged to Jetta. "CLIF-FORD,
COME BACK. WE NEED YOU!"
she called.

 # A Red Speck

A red speck appeared in the distance. Everyone on the boat knew what that red speck was. It was Clifford! Clifford swam closer and closer. The big red dog finally reached the boat. A pod of dolphins swam beside him.

Clifford was glad to see Emily
Elizabeth and the rest of the
children.

Emily Elizabeth pointed in the
direction of the trapped whale.
"Go, Clifford," she said. "The
whale needs your help."

Emily hoped that Clifford would understand what she wanted him to do. She pointed again and said, "Go!"

Clifford turned his head. He turned toward the direction of Emily Elizabeth's finger. But dogs don't have very good eyesight. He didn't understand.

Clifford sniffed. He smelled
animals in trouble. He listened. He
heard the sounds of animals in
trouble. Clifford swam toward the
smells and the sounds. And then
he understood what was happen-
ing. Two animals needed his help.

Clifford grabbed the net
between his teeth and gently
pulled it.

Nothing happened. Clifford
pulled again. Nothing happened.

Clifford pulled again—a little
harder this time—and Happy was
free! She swam to her baby.

Mother and baby leaped with joy. And together they came down with a giant splash.

Clifford barked, and the whales leaped again. Clifford followed them and made a big splash of his own. He was glad to have two new friends.

The whale watchers cheered.
"Hooray for Clifford! Hooray for
Happy! Hooray for Happy's
baby!" The two whales dived and
did not come up near the ferry
again. But Clifford followed the
ferry all the way to the pier.

The big yellow bus was waiting
for Miss Carrington's class.

"I don't want to ride back to
school on a boring old yellow
bus," said Jetta. "I want to ride on
Clifford."

All the boys and girls agreed.

"It's okay with me if it's okay with you," Miss Carrington said to Emily Elizabeth.

"It's okay with me if it's okay with Clifford," said Emily Elizabeth.

She looked at Clifford. His tail was wagging. "It's okay with him," said Emily Elizabeth. "Lie down, Clifford."

Clifford lay down so that Miss Carrington and the children could climb up on his back. And everyone rode back on the big red dog who had saved the whales.

A True Story

Clifford Saves the Whales is based upon an event that really happened. A whale-watching boat called the *Dolphin VI* set off from Province-town, Massachusetts, in 1983. The boat reached Stellwagen Bank, an area known to attract whales— especially humpback whales. About one hundred fifty people on the *Dolphin VI* saw a fishing boat lower its net into the water and trap three whales. One of the whales was hanging upside down with its tail out of the water and its head way down in the water.

The captain of the whale-watching boat tried to reach the fishing boat by radio.

"This is *Dolphin VI*," the captain said. "You have three endangered animals inside your net."

No one in the fishing boat replied. A scientist aboard the *Dolphin VI* told the whale watchers that the whales would drown if they couldn't come up for air. He also explained that to save the whales, the fishermen would have to cut their net. This would be a big problem for the fishermen. They wouldn't be able to catch the fish they had been hoping to catch that day. They would lose money. Cutting the net would cause them great hardship. But humpback whales are endangered animals. Not many are left on Earth. If people don't protect them, every single humpback could die. The species would be gone forever.

Much time had passed, and the captain of the *Dolphin VI* still hadn't heard from anyone on the fishing boat. The whale watchers feared for the lives of the whales.

"Cut the net! Cut the net!" the whale watchers shouted.

Finally, two fishermen entered the water on a rubber raft. They carefully cut their net and saved the lives of the whales. The fishermen gave up their day's work so the whales could go free.

About Whales

Many years ago, people believed
that whales were fish. Like fish,
whales live in water, they swim,
and they have no legs. But whales
are not fish. Fish breathe with
gills. They can stay underwater for
their whole lives. Fish can't
breathe air. But whales have lungs,
like people. Whales must come
to the surface for air.
A whale breathes
through a blowhole
on the top of its head.

There are about seventy-seven different kinds of whales, dolphins, and porpoises. Some whales have teeth. Others have baleen instead of teeth. Baleen acts as a strainer. A baleen whale opens its mouth and lets in lots of water, fish, and krill. The whale pushes the water out through its baleen and swallows what is left.

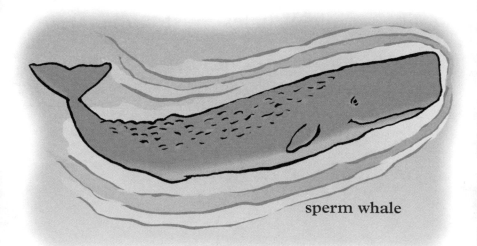

sperm whale

blue whale

Blue whales, gray whales, right whales, and humpback whales have baleen. Sperm whales, killer whales, beluga whales, dolphins, and porpoises have teeth.

The largest whales are the blue whales. They can be as long as 100 feet and weigh up to 150 tons. Blue whales can eat about four tons of krill a day.

Where the Whales Are

Whale watching is now a popular pastime. People take tours on boats—both big and small. Or they watch from lookout points on land. Whales can be seen along both coasts of North America and South America. In Europe, whales can be seen off the shores of France, Portugal, and Greece. They can also be seen off of Hawaii, in South Africa, Sri Lanka, Japan, Australia, New Zealand, and Antarctica.